Emoji Adventures #3

Call of Doodie

ISBN 978-0692655078

#CouchPotatoes

 "Hey, out of my way!"

"Did you just shoot me?"

"Wait... I'm lost."

"Run! Run!"

Dot, Billy, Kevin, and I are enjoying our favorite pastime: sitting in front of the TV, playing every video game we can get our hands on.

"You killed me!" Kevin yells to Dot.

"That's what happens to people who stand in my way," Dot says without looking up.

My father appears in the doorway. "What's all this complaining?"

"Kevin's being a sore loser because Dot's whooping him," Billy smirks.

"That is *not* true," Kevin says.

He's about to keep arguing but my dad cuts him off.

"You kids spend all your time cooped up in here," he says. "When I was your age I used to spend as much time as I could outdoors - ever heard of it?"

"Of course!" Dot says.

I roll my eyes. "He's kidding."

"But I'm serious about all this time inside," Dad says. "It's not good for you."

He walks over to the TV and turns it off in the middle of the game.

"DAD!!!" Kevin and I shout.

"Mr. Emoji!!!" Dot and Billy cry.

"That's how serious I am," Dad says. "You kids have given me an idea. Why don't you play an *outdoor* video game?"

"What's an outdoor video game?" Billy asks.

My dad smiles. "Why, an outdoor video game can be anything you want! Go-kart race? You can do that! Fencing battle? Ski competition? Fairy tournament? Rock concert? You name it, you can do it!"

"How?" I ask.

"By using the best technology of all: your imaginations," Dad says.

We all groan.

"That's just playing outside," I whine.

"Really?!" Dad taps into his phone. "Because I just applied to get that idea patented."

"Maybe we *could* make our own video game," Dot says.

Billy jumps in. "Yeah! We can film ourselves doing all the action then edit the footage!"

"That," Dad says, "is a *really* good idea."

"Let's do it!" we all shout.

There's nothing like a video game to get the old imagination going.

#YouWantUsToWhat

The next day I wake up to loud knocking at my bedroom door.

"Annie! Rise and shine!"

It's Dad, dressed in hiking gear and carrying his camera. He already has way too much energy for me.

"Are you ready?" he asks.

8

"I won't be ready to do anything but sleep for another three hours!" I yawn. "Ready for what?"

"To shoot this video game, of course."

"That was Billy's idea!" I say. "You're not invited."

"Well, too late," he replies, "because I've already rented all the equipment and mapped out our day. I have big hopes for this one. C'mon, up and at 'em!"

I'd like to sleep in, but when my father has a plan, there's no negotiating. Within half an hour we're driving into the woods on the outskirts of Emojiville with a trunk full of various construction supplies.

"What are those for?" Kevin asks.

"You'll see," Dad responds.

We finally arrive at a trailhead where Dot, Billy, Tiffany, Zoe, and Austin are waiting.

"You invited kids from my class?" I ask Dad.

"Of course," he replies. "We have *way* too much work for just the four of us."

Dad, Mr. Ultimate Businessman, spends the next twenty minutes going over contracts and releases he wants all of us to sign.

"I'm not sure they can be signing legal contracts without their parents," Mom says.

"Last time I signed a contract for your Dad," Billy says, "I ended up on a billion people's phones. So count me in!"

"Their parents already signed them last night," Dad adds. "Now we need each child's signature."

Everyone signs the releases and waits for instructions. I can tell Dad is excited for this production, and who knows - maybe it'll be fun after all.

"Alright, kids," Dad says. "Now it's time for us to build the obstacle course."

"What?!" Kevin cries.

"Does not compute," SAM agrees.

"Look, our video game backdrop isn't going to build itself," Dad counters. "And besides, building is half the fun."

"Yeah, right." Tiffany rolls her eyes. "Can't someone else do it?"

Dad shakes his head. "The whole reason this even came about is because you kids spend too much time sitting

around in front of screens. Today,

everyone gets to exercise!"

I put on my patented

smile and prepare to work.

#PreProduction

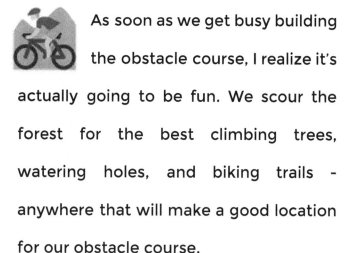 As soon as we get busy building the obstacle course, I realize it's actually going to be fun. We scour the forest for the best climbing trees, watering holes, and biking trails - anywhere that will make a good location for our obstacle course.

As it is, the forest is already an obstacle course - we have barbed wire fences to crawl under and narrow bridges to cross. And that's just to get from one part of the woods to another.

Dad would start filming us now if we'd let him.

"This place is a goldmine!" he calls to no one in particular.

"Watch out for ticks!" Tiffany yells. "I'll be at the picnic tables if anybody needs me."

Dot maneuvers herself up a tree, a bundle of rope over her shoulder. Her climbing gear jingles around her belt as she climbs higher.

"You look really cool up there," Kevin says as he and Billy watch Dot scale the tall pine.

Dot is the best climber of us all, so she gets the most dangerous and fun jobs, which makes everyone - especially the boys - jealous. But fair is fair and I cheer Dot on.

"Safety first!" Dad calls.

"Can you tie this rope around that tree trunk?" Kevin asks Billy.

It's usually a bad idea to help Kevin with anything, but Billy does. He takes the rope from Kevin and walks over to the tree trunk. Just as he's almost there, the ground gives way under him. It's a hole that Kevin must have dug and covered with a thin sheet of leaves.

"AAAH!" Billy hollers as he falls. "Man down!"

"SAM, did you get that?" Kevin laughs hysterically.

"Affirmative," SAM reports.

"That was so funny!" Dot laughs from the tree. "You're so clever, Kevin."

"Just focus on not falling!" I yell to Dot, throwing a rope down to help Billy.

We keep our eyes open for more of Kevin's pranks while we finish building the course.

Several of us are disappointed we're not playing video games, but it's hard not to enjoy such a gorgeous afternoon in the woods. Construction's done and before we know it, our obstacle course is ready to go.

Dad looks like he's about to burst. "Let's get Epic!"

I roll my eyes. Sometimes Dad tries
too hard.

● ●

#DivideAndConquer

Now that construction is finished, everyone is ready for a break. But that's not what Dad has in mind.

"Moving right along!" he calls from his megaphone. "Time is money!"

"At this rate, we'd better make millions," Tiffany says.

"I'm happy with free Craft Services." Austin shovels candy bars from the snack table into his pocket. Zoe looks on and laughs.

We assemble in front of Dad so he can give us directions. I stand next to Dot and Billy to ensure I don't end up on Kevin's team. I reach for my phone to check the time but it's gone. A typical prank by Kevin and SAM.

Seeing me search my pockets, Billy elbows me and points to Kevin who's standing behind the other kids taking photos of cow patties - with my phone.

Dot and Zoe laugh while I wrestle my phone out of his hands.

"Quiet on the set!" Dad calls from the director's chair. I try to be upbeat but between Kevin's pranks and Dad's beret and megaphone, the day is already going downhill.

"In order to film our video game, we're going to split into two teams," Dad says. "Kevin, you'll be the captain of one team and Annie, you'll be the captain of the other."

Nothing like Dad playing favorites by making his two kids captains. Not to mention that Kevin will do anything to beat me. Anything. My heart sinks, but I keep the smile on my face so no one can tell. (That's kinda my thing.)

I know everyone will want to be on Kevin's team, because who wants to play against a cheating, pranking devil? But it looks like I don't have a choice. Kevin and I join Dad in front of our friends and get ready to choose teams.

"Kevin! Kevin! Pick me!" Zoe calls out.

"Maybe," Kevin says.

Zoe giggles at my brother's not-funny joke.

"No, pick me!" Tiffany says.

"No, me!" Dot calls.

"No, *me!*" Billy cries.

Wait - even my two best friends want to be on Kevin's team? I'm insulted, but understand; I'm not an athlete, I'm not competitive, I'm not a pranking devil. Even *I* don't want to be on my team.

"I pick Austin." Kevin chooses the one person who didn't ask to be picked. I'm sure there's a lesson in there somewhere.

"I pick Dot," I say quickly.

I expect Dot to be disappointed she's not with Kevin, but she joins me cheerfully.

"Sorry I asked to be on Kevin's team," she whispers. "He just looks so cute today."

Dot never gets that my brother is evil.

"I pick Zoe," Kevin says.

"Yes!" Zoe giggles.

"What?! No one picks Zoe before me." Tiffany looks at me with daggers in her eyes. "You'd better pick me next."

"Sorry, but I pick Billy," I say.

Billy skips over while Tiffany fumes. (When Billy fumes, it is VERY unpleasant.)

"I knew you'd pick me next," he whispers.

"Are you serious?!" Tiffany yells. "The most popular girl in school picked last? I don't think so. I quit!"

"Phew!" Dad says. "That evens out the teams. Tiffany, you can be my assistant director."

"That's more like it," Tiffany says.

"Okay, everyone," Dad says. "Are you ready to play some paintball?"

Paintball?!

#GroundRules

Dad passes out safety equipment to both teams: goggles, chest protectors, helmets, and elbow pads - all color coordinated to match our teams. My team - the Tigers - gets all the blue gear. Kevin's team - the Skulls - gets the red.

Dad's about to give us our paintball guns but I stop him.

"Kevin will *obviously* try to shoot me before the game even starts," I explain. "You have to make sure he doesn't."

"Anyone who fires their paintball gun before the game starts will forfeit any prize money."

That ought to keep Kevin in check.

Kevin's eye twitches and he hands his gun to SAM.

"He doesn't even trust himself to follow the rules," Billy says.

"That's so endearing," Dot sighs.

Kevin stares at his paintball gun then moves to the other side of Austin.

I'm excited and a little nervous, although I won't let anyone else know.

"This is a wild version of Capture the Flag," Dad begins. "Each team will start at opposite ends of the obstacle course. You will then work your way to your opponent's side and capture the team flag. Don't forget: every player will have a paintball gun with a unique paintball color. If you get hit by three different paintballs, you head to the archery range, and if you can't get a bullseye, you're out of the game."

"Do we need to bring the flags all the way back to our home camp?" Billy asks.

"No, you don't," Dad says. "The first team to get their flag wins the game."

We look at each other as if to say 'piece of cake'.

"That may sound easy," Dad says when he sees our expressions. "But it won't be. I've made sure this is a *difficult* obstacle course."

He's not kidding. I look around at the course we just built and gulp. There's a rope swing, a mud pit, a rock wall, a bridge which looks unstable, and an archery range. Knowing Dad, there are several obstacles we DON'T know about too.

"Number one," Dad says. "No shortcuts. If you take a shortcut, your whole team is disqualified. Got that?"

We all nod.

"Number two. No crossing outside the boundaries of the obstacle course. If you do, your whole team is disqualified.

Everyone got that?"

We nod again.

"Number three. This entire forest is full of hidden cameras I installed yesterday and there are cameras in your helmets, too. Everything - and I mean *everything* - will be recorded. Get it? Got it? Good!"

I can see Kevin's chomping at the bit for Dad to finish so we can play. He shakes his hands, eager for a paintball gun to be in it.

"Is everyone ready?" Dad leads us to the starting line.

"YEAH!!!" we all shout.

"Okay," he smiles. "One, two, three...GO!"

1 **2** **3**

#TigersVsSkulls

 Dot, Billy, and I sprint to the end of the obstacle course with our equipment in hand. I glance over my shoulder to ensure Kevin doesn't shoot me in the back and see him strapping on his gun and running in the other direction.

There's no time to waste; we begin our first obstacle, the fence climb.

Dot goes first, scrambling up the fence so quickly I can't believe it. We're sure to win with such an amazing athlete on our team. But by the time it's my turn, I'm less convinced. When I finally make it over the fence, I'm already exhausted.

"Come on, guys!" Dot says. "We've got this!"

Next is the rope course, which Dot again crosses quickly. Billy goes next, maintaining a close second but I, on the other hand, get so tangled up in the ropes that Dot has to climb back and help me. As she untangles me, I get pelted by the first paintball of the game.

"Gotcha!" a voice yells from a distance. The entire forest echoes with laughter.

It's Zoe from all the way across the field. She strikes Dot in the shoulder next. Who knew Zoe was such a great shot?

The game has barely begun and we've already been hit twice. We finish the rope course and climb over two sets of cargo nets and two wooden walls before arriving at the dilapidated bridge.

This time, Dot and Billy insist I go first; they'd rather have the slowest at the beginning than the end. I go as quickly as I can, but my lack of balance and the unstable bridge prove to be a lethal combination. Only a few steps in, the whole thing tips over and I fall into the icy, murky water.

Billy helps me out and Dot tries to cross next. She makes it halfway but falls in too. I'm almost relieved - I was beginning to feel bad about holding our team back.

"This is impossible!" Dot says. "You're up, Billy!"

"I'm not sure about this," Billy complains.

I can't blame him - I'd want to stay dry if I could too.

"We have two more bridges to cross after this one." Billy points up the trail.

"What if we took this path instead?" I point to a trail hidden behind some shrubs. "It looks like it leads around the lake. It's a shortcut!"

"That would be cheating!" Dot says.

"Think about who we're playing against!" I say. "There's no way Kevin will play fair. He's probably cheated twice already."

Dot looks between the trail and the bridge, clearly torn.

"C'mon, Dot," Billy urges. "No one will ever know we cheated."

"I don't want to fall into that water again." Dot shudders and finally agrees

We take off down the hidden trail quietly to ensure we're not seen by the other team - or the cameras. At first, the trail runs alongside the lake but after a few minutes turns into a dense forest.

"Are you sure we're going the right way?" Dot asks a few minutes later.

"Um... yeah?" I look to Billy for encouragement.

"I hope so," Billy says.

"HOPE so?" Dot says. "I'm in it to win it!"

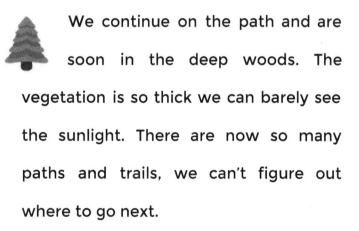 We continue on the path and are soon in the deep woods. The vegetation is so thick we can barely see the sunlight. There are now so many paths and trails, we can't figure out where to go next.

"Where are we?" I ask, as if either of my friends know the answer.

Billy checks the GPS on his phone. "No service!"

"We never should have cheated," Dot says.

"What do we do?" I ask.

A loud rumble and roar can be heard several yards away.

"Try and survive," Billy answers.

#Lost

We've been wandering around the woods for hours and I've already cried twice. I've never been so scared. Twigs snap in the distance and I swear it must be Bigfoot.

"What's that pit?" I point to a small hole at the foot of a tree.

"Looks like a coyote made that," Billy says.

I want to crawl in a hole - although not *that* hole.

"We probably have two more hours of daylight," Billy says. "Three if we're lucky. Do either of you have flashlights?"

"Nope," Dot says.

"Me neither," I say.

"Well, let's hope we figure out a way out soon," Billy says. "Or we'll be camping with the wildlife tonight."

A shiver runs down my spine and I feel like I might cry again.

"My feet hurt," I complain, trying to get my mind off how scared I am.

"Psst! Quiet, you guys. Stay still." Dot suddenly stops.

We all freeze.

"Is that a bear?" Dot whispers. I can't see where she's pointing because my eyes are shut so tightly they may never open again.

"False alarm," she says after an eternity. "Just a tree."

I breathe a sigh of relief, even though we're still not out of the woods. Literally.

After more walking, Billy freezes and I'm worried we might have another animal on our hands. "Wait!" he says.

I look around, but all I see are more trees. Dot, equally confused, shrugs.

"Moss!" Billy exclaims.

Dot and I still have no idea what he's talking about.

"Moss will help us figure out where we are," Billy says, exasperated. "I can't believe I didn't think of this earlier!"

He examines several mossy trees.

"People think the mossy side is always the northern side of the tree."

Billy sounds more like a teacher than a pile of poop. "But in fact, what moss really indicates is moisture."

"What are you talking about?" I ask.

"If we look for the moss on the trees, we can find our way back to the lake where the bridge was," he explains.

"How do you know all this?" Dot asks.

"I've been a Boy Scout all my life, remember?"

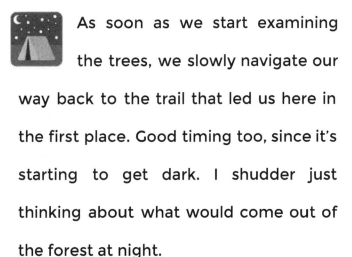 As soon as we start examining the trees, we slowly navigate our way back to the trail that led us here in the first place. Good timing too, since it's starting to get dark. I shudder just thinking about what would come out of the forest at night.

Soon we hear the lapping of the water - we're back at the lake, only this time we pop out near the start of the course. We're only a few yards away and

I'm so excited to see everyone when I hear yelling.

"CHEATERS!!!" Kevin shouts.

We were lost in the woods, scared out of our wits, and all Kevin wants to focus on is the fact that we took a shortcut?

"I was so worried!" Mom cries. "Annie, why didn't you follow the rules? Kevin would never cheat!"

"Kevin *always* cheats," I say.

Dad doesn't seem mad at all. "Between the footage from the hidden cameras and your helmet-cams, we got some great shots!"

I can't believe my ears. "You were watching us the whole time we were lost? While we were scrambling for our lives?"

Dad waves me off. "You were never in harms way - you were fine!" He claps his hands together. "I think we have an awesome video game on our hands!"

I don't know whether to be insulted that Dad wasn't worried or relieved he's not mad.

"Well, thanks for going out of bounds because you made it really easy for us to capture the flag," Austin says.

It's the most Austin has ever spoken to me since Tiffany's birthday party.

"And who do you think got MVP?" Kevin adds. "You guessed it - ME!"

"It's true," Dad says. "The main character gets the biggest share of the profits so good work, Kevin!"

I'll never take a shortcut again.

#PostProduction

Dad spends the next week turning the footage from the obstacle course into a video game. He's so invested in this project, he thankfully has overlooked the fact that I cheated. His happiness is contagious; everyone eagerly anticipates the game and no one talks about how the *real* game ended.

Finally Dad invites Kevin and me into his office to see the rough cut. I gasp as soon as I enter; he's turned his office into a Hollywood-style editing studio, with state-of-the-art video equipment and monitors. He did all this to get us away from our *old* video games?

Seeing how professional Dad's studio is, I'm even more excited to see what he's made.

"Here it is," he says proudly.

He hits 'play,' leaning back in his swivel chair.

The video starts with footage of Dot scaling the fence. In person, her speed and strength were impressive enough; on screen though, she looks like a female Rambo. I'm a little jealous because she looks so heroic, but I'm happy to see my friend shine.

Then there's a shot of Billy in the woods. "We'll follow the moss!" He says bravely, sounding like Indiana Jones. He *also* looks heroic.

"Follow me to safety," he says confidently.

A title card appears: *SOME WILL RISE.*

Next is a shot of Zoe taking aim and firing her paint gun - probably at me - and looking totally cool. Austin's in the background, gazing at her with admiration.

After that is an annoying shot of Kevin on the rope swing, taking it from one side of the creek to the other. Sure, he may carry out the whole procedure with perfect grace, but there's no way around the fact that he's having fun showing off.

"Don't you wish *you* could do that?"
Kevin whispers.

"Whatever," I say.

The trailer cuts back to Billy in the woods. "We have only a few hours left of daylight," he says. "Hey, stop crying!"

The camera turns to show the crying person: me! I look *awful* - crying, whining, and afraid.

Kevin busts out laughing.

"Dad!" I say. "You can't leave this in!"

"What are you talking about?" Dad replies. "It's relatable! Every adventure game needs a character who has a hard time keeping up."

"And that's supposed to be me?"

Another title card appears: *SOME WILL FALL.*

 Now the trailer cuts to a shot of me getting pelted by Zoe's paintball...over and over in slow motion.

"*Owwwwwwwwwww*," I drawl in slo-mo.

As if this weren't enough, there's *another* shot of me, this time talking to Billy and Dot.

"Let's do it," I say. "No one will ever know we cheated."

Kevin nearly falls over with laughter. "Caught red-handed!"

"The hidden cameras got that too?"

I've have never ever been so humiliated in my life.

"Isn't it great?" Dad asks when the trailer is over. "So much action! So much emotion!"

"You made me the worst character in the game!"

"Well, you *were* the worst character in the game." He says it so casually, I can tell he doesn't realize it's an insult. "Did I show you the box yet?"

He excitedly picks up the box from his desk. *CALL OF DOODIE.* It shows all my friends in a lineup looking like action heroes - even Tiffany, who didn't even play.

"I didn't make the cover?" I ask, horrified.

"Of course you did!" Dad says. "You're right there."

He points behind a tree in the background - my face is peeking out and I'm crying again.

Beside me, Kevin himself is crying - with laughter. He leans against Dad's desk for support.

I thought I'd already learned my lesson - that is, not to cheat. But now I've learned another lesson: never work to with Dad.

#TestRun

 Despite my initial shock at the humiliating trailer, I still agree to try out the demo, mostly because I'm hoping my character gets a chance to redeem herself. My opponent is Kevin who relishes the opportunity.

"I hope you don't start crying when we play," he says as we take our seats in the living room. "There are enough tears in the video to fill a swimming pool."

"Leave me alone," I reply.

Dad turns on the game, which starts with an amazing shot of the obstacle course.

"Cool!" Kevin and I agree for one of the few times in our lives.

We pick our avatars - ourselves, of course - and start the game. On one side of the screen I walk around the forest, looking at the trees. On the other side of the screen, Kevin walks around the forest while Dot walks towards the lake.

"How do we get to the obstacle course?" Kevin asks Dad.

"You have to figure it out!" Dad says, grinning.

Five minutes later, our avatars are still wandering around the forest. It feels a lot like the situation Billy, Dot, and I were in the other day, although this time around, the direction of the moss doesn't help. Not to mention that as a video game, wandering around the forest is pretty boring.

"Dad, you might want to make it a little easier to find the obstacle course," I suggest.

"What, and spoil all the fun?" Dad asks. "No way!"

But it *isn't* fun. Finally I find the obstacle course - before Kevin! - but as soon as I do, I can't get the paintball gun out of my hands. I try to climb the fence, but instead shoot myself in the foot.

"Dad, this game doesn't make any sense!" Kevin says angrily. He still hasn't found the obstacle course.

I somehow make it up the fence but shoot myself five times in the process. Perched on top of the fence, my avatar can see Kevin from above. Now's the perfect chance for revenge! I lift my paintball gun, take aim and... start crying. Not in real life: my *avatar* starts crying.

"Dad!" I say. "You made it impossible for me to play!"

"*You* made it impossible," Dad says cheerfully. "The game just reflects that."

"This game stinks." Kevin puts his controller down.

"I agree."

"Don't be spoilsports," Dad says. "Be at the launch party at the game store tomorrow and I'll prove you wrong. You'll want to be there when this game becomes the Next Big Thing."

More like the Next Lame Thing.

#LaunchParty

Mom makes us arrive early at the *Call of Doodie* party to set up decorations in a fiesta theme. We spend hours hanging pinatas and blowing up balloons. Even though I don't like Dad's game, I still want to be supportive so I hang streamers and smile.

It looks like Mom spent a lot of time preparing. I'm horrified to see the pinatas are in the shape of the video game characters - us! I want to beat the crying Annie pinata but don't because Mom spent hours making it.

There is a taco truck outside and a special burrito called the "Crying Commando" named after me. It comes with extra napkins and onions and is sure to make you cry. Very funny.

There are free hats, a photo booth, and a bunch of stations where people can test the game.

Lots of kids show up to test it, including all my friends. The newspaper and local tv stations are here too. Even though Dad releases a new invention every season, they still always show up. (Emojiville can get pretty quiet, so the media will take any story they can get.)

I try to avoid the play test area as long as possible. I don't want to be anywhere near the horrifying footage of me whining and crying. My curiosity finally gets the best of me, however, and I sneak over to eavesdrop on people's conversations as they play:

"I can't find the obstacle course!"

"I accidentally used all my ammo!"

"My character keeps crying and trying to cheat - how do I switch?"

Ouch.

"This game is horrible!" someone shouts, saying what everyone else is thinking.

"Totally uncool," Austin says.

"No laughing matter," Zoe agrees.

As much as I'm glad not to be the game's scapegoat, I'm disappointed for Dad. He spent so much time working on this, but I'd be surprised if anyone bought it. Ever.

I hide out in the back room until the end of the party, embarrassed to be seen. Soon there's no one left in the store but my family. Dad looks defeated.

"No one bought my game!" Dad says. "Not even Mom."

"Whoops," Mom says, her rosy cheeks getting redder.

"My inventions always fail," Dad moans. "All this hard work amounted to nothing."

"But Dad," I say. "You can fix this! You have a ton of amazing footage - you just need a different programmer to put it together into a better game."

"Where am I going to find a new programmer on such short notice?" Dad asks. "I've got a second launch party next week."

"I know a few editing tricks," I say confidently.

"I do too," Kevin adds. "And there's always SAM."

I'm reluctant to work with my devilish brother and his annoying robot but I'll do anything for our family.

"What do you have to lose, Dad?" I ask.

"She's right," Mom chimes in.

Dad reluctantly agrees.

"It'll be great," Kevin says.

I'm excited; I've always wanted to program a game and can finally put the skills I learned at App Camp to good use.

Plus, this is just the opportunity I need to save my avatar from further humiliation.

#PostPostProduction

That night Kevin and I get to work tweaking the game. The problems are clear: it takes too long to find the obstacle course, it's too easy to accidentally shoot paintball pellets, and it's hard to figure out the game's objective. Oh, and another problem: my character is an annoying crybaby.

As soon as we start using Dad's editing software, it's clear Kevin is a LOT better than I am at programming. I shouldn't be surprised; after all, SAM wouldn't exist to drive me crazy if it weren't for Kevin's masterful way with computers. The thought of SAM makes me check my pocket to make sure he hasn't stolen my phone again.

I try to fix the paintball gun firing problem but fail miserably, shooting my own avatar in the foot several times. The best I can do is add funny "OOPS!" sound effects whenever the paintball guns go off accidently. Which is often.

Kevin, meanwhile, immediately fixes the course-finding problem and reprograms the game so it starts on the actual obstacle course. I guess all those hours of staring at the computer screen have paid off for him. SAM tackles the paintball gun problem I couldn't fix.

"Kevin, I'm really impressed!" I say. I'm not used to giving him compliments, but I'm proud of him today.

"Maybe you should take five and let the pros deal with this," he responds.

Kevin and SAM spend the next two days locked in the editing studio, working as hard as they can to fix Dad's game.

"I'm a little concerned," I say to Mom and Dad. "Kevin didn't even leave the room when the ice cream truck went by."

 "Freckles is worried too," Mom says, pointing to the cat. "She's been laying by the door to the studio all day."

I get a text from Dot: "Any word on the game? That's so sweet of Kevin!"

I know she's only asking because she has a crush, but I appreciate her concern anyway.

"What if the game is still bad after all this?" Dad asks.

"I'm not concerned about the game. I'm worried about Kevin."

"Don't worry about him," Mom says, smiling. "I've been bringing him meals and his favorite snacks the whole time. And besides, he can fix any problem he sets his mind to. "

I'm about to tell her that hasn't exactly been *my* experience with Kevin,

but suddenly the door to Dad's office

swings open.

"We have ourselves a game,"

Kevin says.

#ReLaunch

Now that Kevin has spruced up Dad's game, it's time to re-launch the project. The game shop allows Dad a chance to redeem himself and lets Mom throw an even bigger party.

"Set up the bounce house and the DJ in the parking lot!" Mom shouts to the staff. "Hang these fish from the ceiling, kids."

Mom goes for a beach bash this time and has us set up inflatable fish and buckets of sand throughout the store. She's even giving out beach towels with the game characters on them. Kids are fighting over who gets the crying Annie towels.

I'm amazed by the turnout the second time around. The crowd is even bigger than at last week's premiere. (Emojiville really *does* get pretty quiet.) All of my friends come back and are eager to see the improvements to the game.

There seems to be one key difference between this party and the last one: the lines to try the demo of the game are moving very slowly. Is it possible it's even harder to play than last time?

But no, copies of the game are flying off the shelves! It seems to be a huge hit.

"We're rich!" Dad puts money into the cash register with a smile.

I can't wait to try the new game. Looks like Kevin really nailed it. Finally I make it to the front of the line and excitedly take my seat in front of the monitor.

"Welcome to *Call of Doodie*," a familiar voice says. It's SAM! What a great idea to have a robot narrate the game. I've got to hand it to Kevin; it looks like he knocked this one out of the park.

"To start," SAM continues. "Check out the map to see all the fun things you can do in Call of Doodie."

After studying the terrain, I test out my paintball gun, which has more features than before. You can still shoot paintballs but who'd want to if the other choices are laser spiderwebs, sharks, rainbows, and even flames? Kevin has really outdone himself.

"Once you've selected the ammo at your disposal, here is your mission," SAM says. "Hunt down and neutralize the target. Navigate the obstacle course. Your enemy can hide, but she can't run...very well!"

She?

Suddenly my crying face appears on the screen, but this time I'm programmed so I'm running away from the player.

"This is hard!," my avatar cries. "I keep falling down!"

What!? I'M the moving target in this game?! Not as strong girl who conquers obstacles, but as a girl who complains and cries? When I find Kevin's avatar, I'm going to clobber him with spiderwebs and flaming rainbows.

I finally get up from the game to track down the real Kevin. I see him across the room, signing copies of the game.

On my way I pass Billy and Dot.

"How's the new game?" Dot asks.

"I'm excited to play."

"It's horrible!" I say.

"Oh no, is there still footage of you crying?" Billy says.

"Worse," I say. "There's twice the amount of footage as last time."

"Look on the bright side," Dot says. "Your hair looks great in the video."

But my great hair is no consolation. I need to give Kevin a piece of my mind. I approach him as he signs a copy of the game for Austin: "Stay cool."

"You embarrassed me in front of the whole town!"

"Embarrassed?" he asks. "This game is the biggest hit of the year!"

"Hey, is that the moving target?" Someone behind him points at me.

"It is!" someone else says. "Let's see if she starts crying!"

The gamers laugh and I race out of the store even faster than my avatar runs through the woods. Billy and Dot try to follow but for once, I'm faster than they are. This time, no one will see me cry.

#LaughingStock

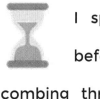 I spend the next two hours before my parents get home combing through the contract we all signed. When my parents walk in, I can feel their excitement about the new game's success.

"Can you believe it?" Dad exclaims. "We sold out! I bet we made the biggest game of the year!"

"You mean *Kevin* made the biggest game of the year," I reply. "All I did was cry and become the laughing stock of Emojiville."

"I always thought Zoe was the laughing stock of Emojiville," Mom says.

"Annie," Dad says softly. "It never occurred to me that this footage would embarrass you."

"Well, it does!" I say. "And I told you that before you released the first game!"

"It's true, she did," Mom says.

"Honey, I'm really sorry," Dad says. "In all this excitement, I didn't listen. I feel awful."

I don't say a word.

"I can't tell what you're thinking because you're still smiling," Dad continues.

"Well," I say finally. "At least your game is a hit. I guess I'm happy for you."

Dad brings me in for a hug.

"What a team player!" he says. "You know what? Just for that, I'm taking you out for ice cream. Just the two of us."

 When we leave the house, the smile on my face is genuine. Not just because of the ice cream, but because I can tell how happy Dad is to have a successful invention again.

#PostPostPostProduction

 Billy and Dot come over the next day to talk about what happened at the party.

"It's so unfair!" Dot complains. "I'd never stand for such humiliation."

Ever since she showed off her athletic skills, Dot has shown a newfound toughness.

"I wish I was as strong as you," I say. "Then this never would have happened in the first place."

"Wait a minute," Billy says. "What if we changed the game before your Dad sends it out for mass production? We'll still have you as the moving target, but we make you as good an athlete as Dot. We could even use some of Dot's footage and place your head on her body!"

"Tell me more."

"This time you'll be scaling fences and swinging on ropes instead of crying and whining like a wimp."

I'm a little insulted by the "wimp" part but otherwise, it's a great idea.

"I'm fine with being the target as long as I'm not the butt of the joke."

The three of us get to work reprogramming Dad's game yet again. He's so busy promoting the game and Kevin is so busy bragging about his success, nobody notices we've taken over the editing studio.

It turns out Billy knows a ton about programming too so he's able to make a game that looks just as good as Kevin's. This time around, the setup is that I'm the target because I'm such an amazing spy.

 "You're like the female, smiley version of James Bond," Kevin says.

Finally, we doctor up a new cover for the game. This time around, I'm front and center, swinging from a vine. I have a bandana around my forehead and a cool little scar on my smiling face.

"No one's gonna think I'm a wimp now," I say.

That evening, I approach Dad in the kitchen to tell him what my friends and I have spent the past week doing. I'm worried he'll be mad, but instead he smiles.

"I felt bad promoting the game once I realized it embarrassed you," he says. "This sounds like a perfect update and - even better - a cash cow!"

I can't wait for everyone to see the new game. Dad and I make a few phone calls to the store as well as some members of the press and get ready for

Launch Party #3.

#BestPartyEver

 Dot, Billy, my family, and I are inside the game store, watching people line up to try out *Call of Doodie: Catch Me If You Can.* I can't believe we're back here for the *third* launch party of this crazy game. Even more unbelievable is that people want more; it's a good thing there are so many couch potatoes here in Emojiville.

Everyone is excited to try out the new game except Kevin who didn't realize we'd changed it until now.

"This is outrageous!" he fumes. "First Annie cheats, then she trashes my game?"

"We didn't trash it," I say. "We improved it."

As if on cue, Dad appears.

"My daughter, the innovator," he says proudly, pointing to the growing 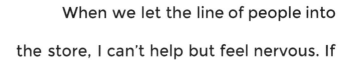 line. "Kevin, this is an even bigger turnout than for your version!"

When we let the line of people into the store, I can't help but feel nervous. If this doesn't pay off, no one's going to trust me with a project like this again.

My curiosity gets the better of me and I walk over to the demo station to see what people think.

"I'll just be a sec!" one of the players says. "I just... have to... finish this level..."

"This new moving target is tough as nails!" another player says.

People can't get enough of the game! The votes are in: it's even better than Kevin's version. I couldn't be more proud or more grateful to my friends.

"Hey, there she is!" someone calls. "The moving target herself!"

"Careful, don't tick her off," someone else says. "You don't want to mess with her."

"Did you hear that?" I ask Kevin.

"Nope," he lies.

Toward the end of the party, Dad approaches, bursting with excitement.

"There's still a line out the door," he says. "Someone took a clip of themselves playing and posted it online. It's going viral."

Billy, Dot, and I look at each other in disbelief.

"The new version has already sold out and is on back-order for the next month!" he says. "This is my biggest hit ever, all thanks to you, Annie!"

Bullseye.

#WinnerTakesAll

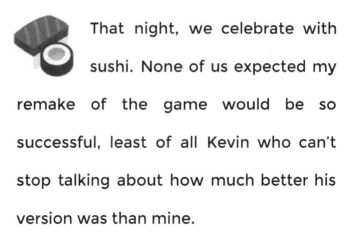 That night, we celebrate with sushi. None of us expected my remake of the game would be so successful, least of all Kevin who can't stop talking about how much better his version was than mine.

Kevin paces the kitchen holding his MVP trophy. "With all the money I'll make off this game, I'm gonna build a *permanent* obstacle course in the backyard. Maybe I'll let you cry all over my course too, Annie."

I let him go on with his plans before finally speaking up.

"Actually, Kevin," I say with my best smile. "You might want to take a look at the fine print in the contract. Because I'm the lead in the final version of the game, I actually get the biggest cut of the profits."

Kevin's expression goes from mischievous to confused. "Dad, what is she talking about?"

"Annie's right," Dad says. "When you made her the target of the game, she became the main character. And the main character gets the big bucks."

"But I have the MVP trophy!" Kevin cries.

"You were MVP of the obstacle course," I reply. "I'm MVP of the video game."

"This is so unfair!"

"Unfair is making your sister the laughing stock of the whole town," I say. "In my opinion, justice was served."

"Perhaps you can share some of your earnings with your brother," Mom suggests.

"We'll see," I say, which is my polite way of saying *no*.   But I do plan on sharing the profits with Dot and Billy. If it weren't for their programming skills, great ideas, and support, I'd still be crying on screen for the world to see.

Dad clears his throat and raises his glass. "I want to make a toast," he says. "To my fearless, brilliant daughter who made the best game ever."

"Cheers!" Mom joins.

"Cheers!" I say, beaming.

"Cheers!" SAM says from the hallway. Even Kevin's robot is on my side.

Kevin looks like he's about to cry. I only wish there was a camera here to film him.

#LeaveUsAReview
Please support us by leaving a review.
The more reviews we get, the more
books we will write.

#FollowUsOnInstagram
@AnnieEmoji * @KevinEmoji

#BooksInTheSeries

Horse Party * Emoji Olympics
Call of Doodie * Reality TV

#MakeaCameo
Want to be a Character in the next Emoji
Adventures Book? Enter at:
www.EmojiAdventuresBook.com

MONTAGE PUBLISHING

www.MontagePublishing.com

Turn the Page!

59653183R00061

Made in the USA
Lexington, KY
11 January 2017